...o se da cuenta porque está muy ocupada sirviend... ...ndig is mod... ...ák voltak. Az egész kör-

los pocos niños que faltan y se muestra muy c... ...hyéken ők hasz... Alig kapok le...

...una niña que está llorando por la cantidad... di quella notte... ...azt... ...banor...

...cho que hay en su so... ...ani Rokavskega preliva. Navzgor... Talán a többi gyere... ablak...

...n muy amabl... ...s po ozki skalnati potki in se spustiš približno... ...ág tévedett, és es... ...pillanat, és ők is megláti... ...anyát és per sco...

...kilometrov po makadamski cesti. Ko prideš... ...emo po... ...t sem bánom, ha mindenki megtudja

...tünk el – jelentette K... ...urcsa! Az aut... ...a je nagrbančil čelo. »Želim si dom... ...is reménykedik maj...

pontosan tudtam, hogy ő mit ak... ...látom világosan... ...ülne ben... zelo bolan. Komaj enajst let je star. Ime mu je jo...

...mikor majd értem jönnek, még... Meg néhány... ...iki mislijo, da ne bo več dolgo živel. Mama...

...ztem akkor is tudni fogják... ...da se vsako noč vročičen p... ...v nacistično taborišče smrt...

...ležal nezavesten, a ti uspe, da se...

...hitim dom... ...elo očala ostanejo cela, tvoja prija...

...bančil čelo. »Želim si domo... ...rbančil čelo. »Želim si dom... ...te sreče in obleži mrtva, zato jo...

...o prekriješ z ni...

...elo bolan. Komaj enajst let je star. Ime mu je... bolan. Komaj enajst let je star. Ime mu je...

...ravniki mislijo, da ne bo več dolgo ži... Mama... ...niki mislijo, da ne bo več dolgo živel. Mama m...

...la, da se vsako noč vročičen... ...vsako noč vročičen prebuja in m...

...bančil čelo. »Želim si domo... ...reno zasmeja...

...bolan. Komaj enajst let je star. Ime mu je Johnlas. Neopisljivo je bila ponosna na svoje...

...verdad. No puedes ten... Zdravniki mislijo, da ne bo več dolgo živel. Mama m... »Kaj pravzaprav počnete...

...creta. Con tus amigos tie... ...pisala, da se vsako noč vročičen prebuja in me klič... ...bi zamenjala temo pog...

...cuando se te escapa una... Moški... ...les has estado contand... ...pisala mi je, naj pohitim domov.«

...Marcelle in Coco sta bili mehkega srca in besed...

...so... ...lo do živega. »Kje ste...

...m, kivéve Ludwik atyá... ...ember ülne... ...t kalózok raboltak el. Aztán anya, hogy vajon három...

...mondani, hogy sees... ...vát is. Méat a haj... ...egy Németországbriernek-e.

...s apa viszont nem olyan nagyon vallásos, figyet... ...ahol azt látt... Tudja... ...milyen az, amikor egy gyere...

...n vágnak neki éjjel az útnak. ...ropokba raktak, és... ...haját vagy kiesik egy foga, és erre a szül...

...kat... ...ndulnak, ha fölkel a nap ...zo lábaiként használták őket. ...t hajtogatják, hogy biztos te vagy a fia a...

...dász... ...ggódom, hogy vaj... ...endben van, elfogadom, hogy a legt... ...ernak, aki ott lakik az utca végén?

...t me... ...ismernek-e. ...eltúlzott, de mégis fölismerik... ...Persze én még ennél is jobban me...

...hogy... ...lyen az, amikor egy gy... ...at, és tudni fogják, hogy... ...és apát látt... ...gyszer egész éjjel ébren voltam, úgy v...

...gy kiesik egy foga, és erre a szül... ...ás, karszalagos férfit ...nya és apa megérkezzék.

...gatják, hogy biztos te vagy a fia annak a su... De nem jöttek.

The Treasure Box

For Gary, the optimist

F. B.

Text copyright © 2013 by Margaret Wild. Illustrations copyright © 2013 by Freya Blackwood.
Published by arrangement with The Penguin Random House Group Limited. All rights reserved.
No part of this book may be reproduced, transmitted, or stored in an information retrieval
system in any form or by any means, graphic, electronic, or mechanical, including photocopying,
taping, and recording, without prior written permission from the publisher.
First U.S. edition 2017. Library of Congress Catalog Card Number pending. ISBN 978-0-7636-9084-7.
This book was typeset in Mrs Eaves. The illustrations were done in pencil, watercolor, and collage.
The text that forms part of the illustrations is taken from foreign editions of
The Silver Donkey by Sonya Hartnett and of *Once* and *Then* by Morris Gleitzman.
Reprinted with kind permission of the authors, Cairo Books, and Carlsen.
Candlewick Press, 99 Dover Street, Somerville, Massachusetts 02144. visit us at www.candlewick.com.
Printed in Humen, Dongguan, China. 17 18 19 20 21 22 APS 10 9 8 7 6 5 4 3 2 1

MIX
Paper from
responsible sources
FSC® C101537
FSC
www.fsc.org

CANDLEWICK PRESS

The Treasure Box

Margaret Wild

illustrated by Freya Blackwood

When the enemy bombed the library, everything burned.

Charred paper, frail as butterflies, fluttered in the wind.
People caught the words and cupped them in their hands.

Only one book survived. A book that
Peter's father had taken home to study.
A book he loved more than any other.

When the enemy ordered everyone out of their
houses, Peter's father brought out a small iron box.
"This will keep our treasure safe," he said.

"But we have no treasure," said Peter. "No rubies, no silver, no gold."

His father wrapped the book in a thick cloth and put it in the box. "This is a book about our people, about us," he said. "It is rarer than rubies, more splendid than silver, greater than gold."

Peter and his father joined the others fleeing the city.
Behind them, their houses burned.

For weeks, they trudged through mud and rain.
They slept at the side of the road, under hedges,
in ditches, huddling together to keep warm.

As the days went by, Peter's father became very ill.
He whispered, "You must be brave, for both of us.
Promise me you will keep our treasure safe."

"I promise," said Peter, and he gripped
his father's hand through the long night.

In the morning, the other people helped Peter bury
his father and say good-bye.
  "Leave the iron box," they told him. "We have a long
way to go."

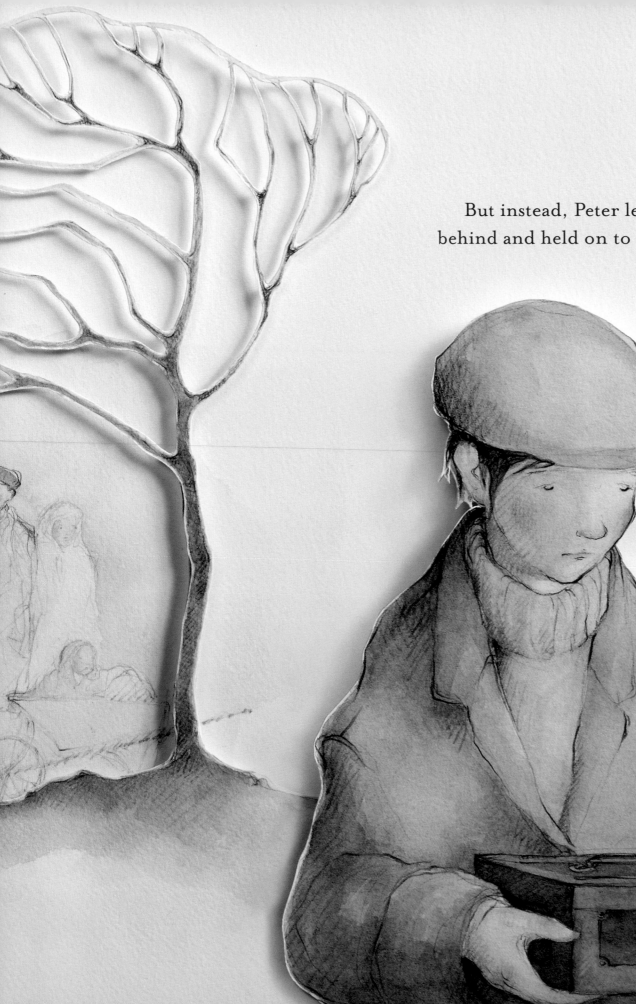

But instead, Peter left his suitcase
behind and held on to the box.

kiderítették
Németországba, ahol azt látták
a könyvellátás
könyveket oszlopokba raktak
lábaiként használták
ezalatt megmentett egy
kalózok raboltak el. Aztán anya és apa együtt
végre itt vagyunk. Az utazásai
után fölismernek
Németországba
játok, milyen az, amikor könyveket oszlopokba
ját vagy kiesik egy fog
szülei egyre
autó dübörög be az udva
hajtogatják, hogy
annak a
és a pizsamám ujjavál
aki ott lakik az
fölismerik
Marektől

By the time he reached the last village, Peter's arms ached.
He knew he would never be able to carry the box over the
mountains.

At the edge of the village was a cottage with
an ancient linden tree.

Peter chipped away at the frozen earth under
the tree and buried the box. Here, it would be
safe from bombs and fire.

During the following years, as Peter grew from a boy to a man in a strange new country, he often thought about his father and the book he'd loved more than any other.

When it was safe to return, he journeyed back
to the cottage at the edge of the village.

He saw a little girl playing in the garden.
He told her about the treasure under the linden tree.

She helped him dig up the iron box.
"Will I see rubies and silver and gold?"
asked the little girl.
Peter opened the box.
"Oh," she said, "it's only a book."

"This is a book about our people, about us," Peter said. "It is rarer than rubies, more splendid than silver, greater than gold."

Peter took the iron box back to the city
where he had lived when he was young.

There was now a new library with new books.

He put the book back on the shelf,
where, once again, it could be found,

and read . . .

and loved.